DAWN

Words and Pictures by URI SHULEVITZ

Farrar, Straus and Giroux   New York

To my parents

Quiet.

Still.

It is cold and damp.

Under a tree by the lake

an old man and his grandson
curl up in their blankets.

The moon lights a rock, a branch, an occasional leaf.

The mountain stands guard, dark and silent.

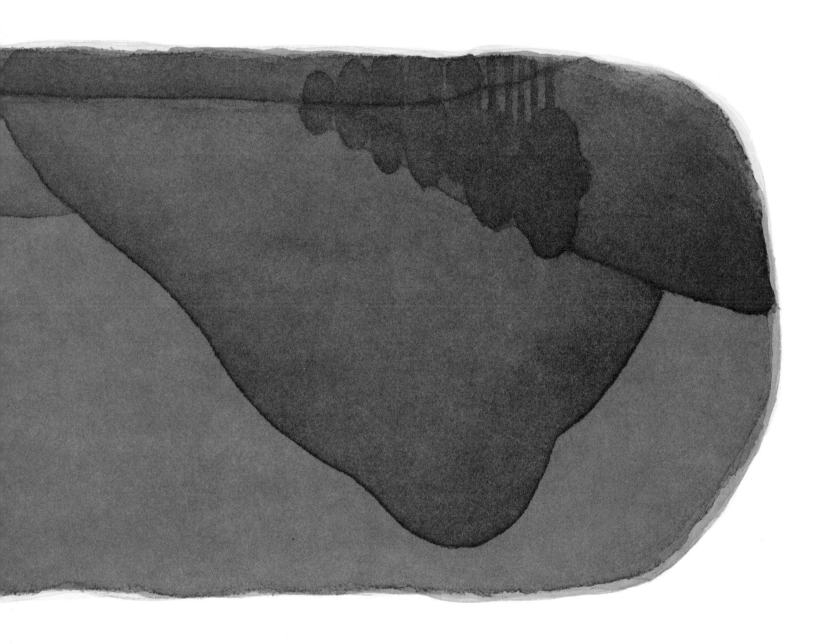

Nothing moves.

Now, a light breeze.

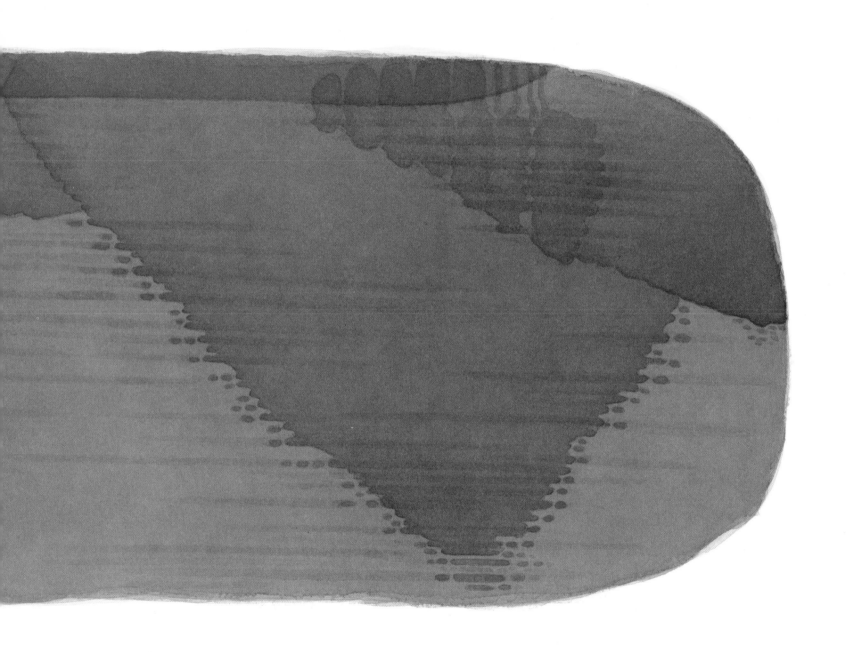

The lake shivers.

Slowly, lazily, vapors start to rise.

A lonely bat circles in silence.

A frog jumps.

Then another.

A bird calls.

Another answers.

The old man wakes his grandson.

They draw water from the lake

and light a small fire.

They roll up the blankets

and push their old boat into the water.

Alone, they move in the middle of the lake.

The oars screak and rattle,
churning pools of foam.

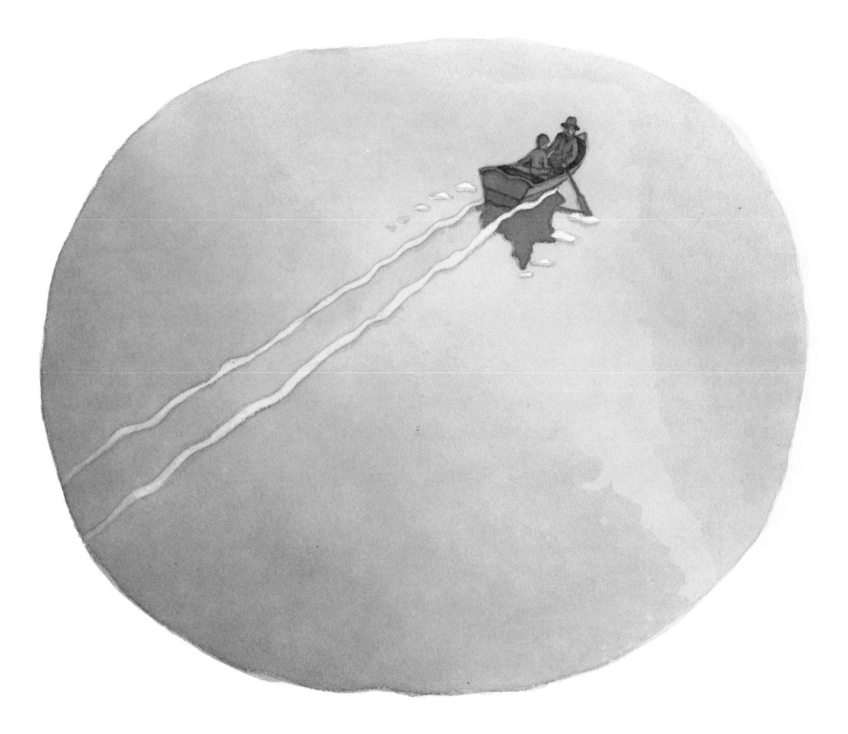

Suddenly

the mountain and the lake are green.

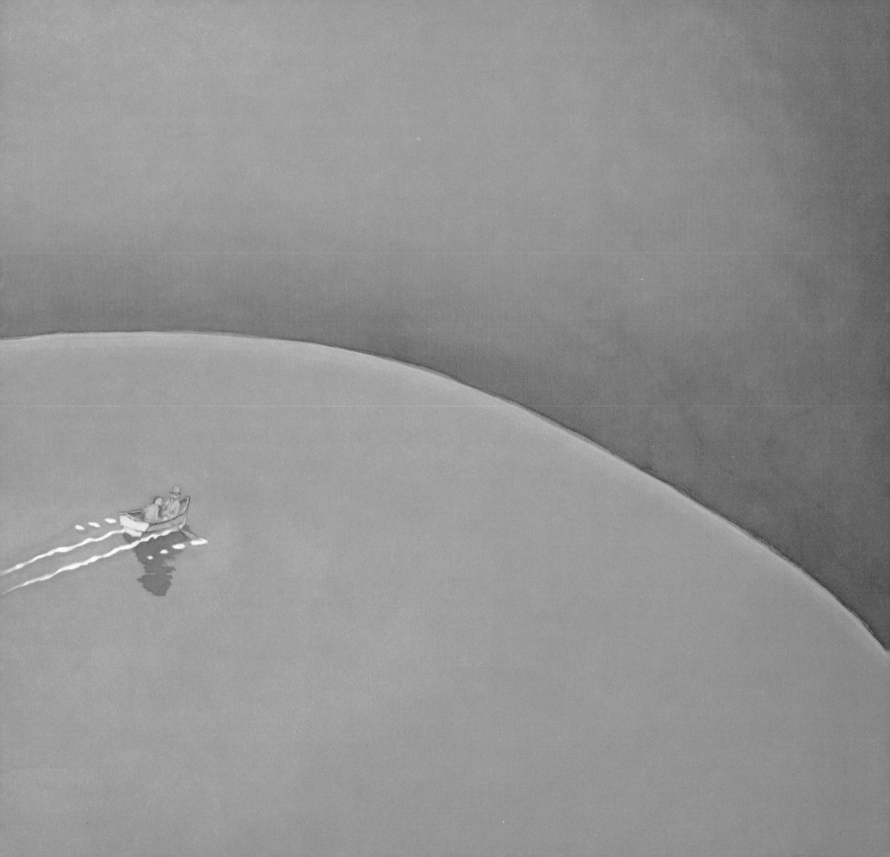